One day Bramble said, "I must water my rose!"
But nothing came out when he turned on the hose.
"That's odd," frowned the badger, scratching his head,
and he went in to make a hot chocolate instead.

The tap in the kitchen just gurgled and spluttered.
"No water here either. Oh dear!" Bramble muttered.

He went to his friends, little Snuffle and Boo.
The taps had stopped working at their houses, too.

As Bramble went homeward, he soon found out why...

The bed of the river was totally dry!

"Oh Bramble," said Tipper the toad, looking grim.
"Where's all the water? I've nowhere to swim!"

"Don't worry," said Bramble. "Leave it to me.
I'm going to follow the river and see."

For ages he followed the dry river bed.
"I hope it's not very much further!" he said.
He came to the place where the giant oak stood
and entered the loneliest part of the wood.

The wood became wilder, the ground became rougher.
The way through the trees became darker and tougher.

He scrambled
through thorns

and he clambered up rocks.

He got tangled in ivy,
and startled a fox.

Two cheeky squirrels gave Bramble a fright,
giggled, and scampered away out of sight.

Bramble chased after them, tripped on a snake,

and ended up – SPLASH!
– in a freezing cold lake.

Onwards he plodded, along the rough track.
He was helping his friends and would never turn back.

He spotted a big heap of wood up ahead.

"No wonder we haven't got water!" he said.

"The river's been blocked by these branches and sticks.

Have those naughty young squirrels been up to their tricks?"

Bramble went closer and gasped, "Goodness me!
A house on an island. Whose can it be?"

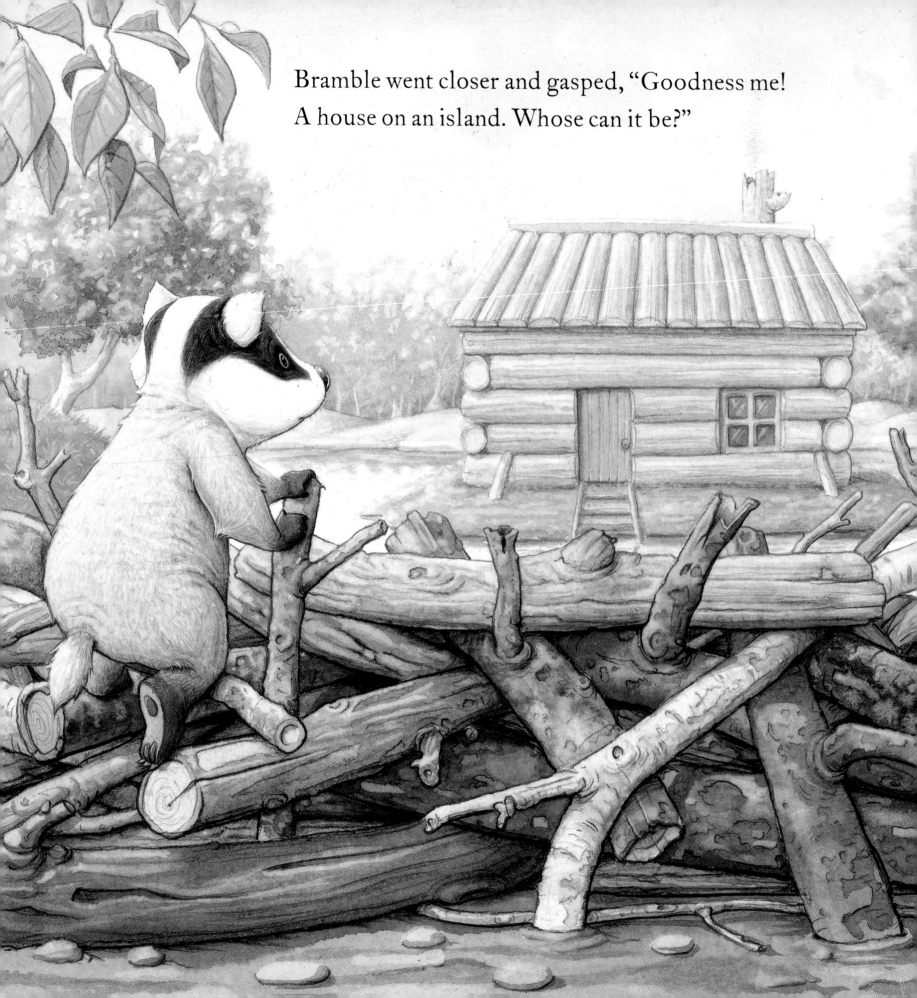

Out of the door popped a sleek, furry head.
"Hello! What creature are you?" Bramble said.
The stranger replied, "I'm a beaver. I'm Sam!
What do you think of my marvellous dam?

This nice lonely river is perfect for me.
My dam can't disturb any neighbours, you see."
"There's no one round here," Bramble said with a frown.
"But you've stopped all the water for folks further down."

"Yikes!" cried the beaver. "Poor creatures! Oh no!
I'll build a new home. But where will I go?"
Bramble said, "Well, there's a place very near.
It's somewhere I stumbled in, on my way here."

He showed Sam the lake. Sam grinned with delight.
"It's perfect!" he said. "I shall move in tonight.
If I build my home here then I won't need a dam.
But first I must take down my old one," said Sam.

Said Bramble, "I'll lend you a paw, if you like.
Then I'd better head home. It's a very long hike."
Sam said, "Oh, I know an easier way.
You won't have to trudge any further today!"

Soon afterwards, down on the riverside track,
Bramble's friends wondered just when he'd be back.
"Listen," said Snuffle. "What's that strange sound?"
"An earthquake?" said Boo, with his ear to the ground.

It came closer and closer – a rumbling and rushing,
a splishing and splashing, a gurgling and gushing.

"The river's come back!" cried Tipper with glee.
"Bramble has done it! But where can he be?"

"Look! There he is!" Snuffle squeaked. And they laughed…

…as Bramble came floating along on a raft!

Said Bramble, "Well, that was a bit of a day!
But I'm pleased that I've made a new chum on the way."
And they all gave a warm friendly welcome to Sam,
then went back to Bramble's for muffins and jam.

For my family - P.B.

For Zephanie, who has a home by a stream - C.F.

The charity Devon Wildlife Trust leads England's
only wild beaver project. To find out more visit
www.devonwildlifetrust.org/river-otter-beaver-trial-appeal